E   Brillhart, Julie.

     The dino expert.

                    472818

$13.95

DATE			
AUG 1 1 1994	JUL 1 7 1996		
SEP 0 1 1994	AUG 0 7 1996		
SEP 2 1 1994	OCT 2 1 1996		
SEP 2 1 1994			
NOV 1 7 1994			
APR 1 5 1995	FEB 1 0 1997		
MAY 1 5 1995	APR 0 9 1997		
JUL 2 0 1995	AUG 1 8 1997		
OCT 3 0 1995	APR 0 4 1998		

THE
DINO EXPERT

Written and Illustrated
by Julie Brillhart

ALBERT WHITMAN & COMPANY, MORTON GROVE, ILLINOIS

To M.H. and D.G.

With special thanks to Dr. Fred Rogers,
Division of Natural Sciences, Franklin Pierce College,
Rindge, New Hampshire, for sharing his expert
knowledge of dinosaurs.

Library of Congress Cataloging-in-Publication Data
Brillhart, Julie.
   The dino expert / Julie Brillhart.
      p.   cm.
   Summary: Five-year-old dinosaur expert Eric feels bad when he
mistakes a great blue heron for a flying pteranodon, until he
discovers the possible relationship between dinosaurs and modern
birds.
   ISBN 0-8075-1597-3 (lib. bdg.)
   [1. Pteranodon—Fiction. 2. Dinosaurs—Fiction.] I. Title.
PZ7. B7666Di   1993
[E]—dc20   92-43474
                                                     CIP
                                                      AC

Text and illustrations © 1993 by Julie Brillhart.
Designed by Karen A. Yops.
Published in 1993 by Albert Whitman & Company,
6340 Oakton Street, Morton Grove, Illinois 60053-2723.
Published simultaneously in Canada
by General Publishing, Limited, Toronto.

Eric was five years old, and he was crazy about dinosaurs!

He had a dinosaur T-shirt and dinosaur shoes and just
about everything there was that had to do with dinosaurs,

and he knew just about everything there was to know
about dinosaurs.

He had gone on a fossil hunt in Utah and seen real
dinosaur footprints!

When he grew up, he was going to study dinosaur bones
and put together huge dinosaur skeletons.

If his friends had questions about dinosaurs, they always asked him. And so did a lot of grownups. Eric was known around town as "the Dino Expert."

Or, as Mrs. Williams, the librarian, liked to say, "the budding paleontologist!"

One spring morning, Eric and his friend Sam were
outside playing. All of a sudden, they heard a loud
squawking noise overhead.

Flying just above them was this HUGE thing with great big flapping wings. They had never seen anything like it before!

"Hey!" cried Eric. "That looks just like a Pteranodon!"
"Wow!" said Sam.
"Come on!" said Eric. "Let's find out!"

They ran up to Eric's room. Eric opened his *Big Book About Prehistoric Life* to the picture of the Pteranodon.

"See," cried Eric, "It looks the same!"

"Yes," said Sam. "We saw a flying Pteranodon!"

Eric was so excited that he leaped from his bed and flew around the room yelling, "Squawk! Squawk! Squawk!"

"Let's go!" he shouted. "We don't want to miss him when he flies by again!"

So off they went outside.

Suddenly Sam stopped running. "But you told me dinosaurs were extinct," he said.

"They are," said Eric. "But this isn't a dinosaur. A Pteranodon is a kind of pterosaur."

"What's a pterosaur?" asked Sam.

"A winged reptile that lived at the same time as the dinosaurs," said Eric.

"Oh," said Sam.

"It's true," said Eric. "I'm the Dino Expert!"

For the rest of the afternoon, they kept a close watch for the Pteranodon. They looked in the sky

and on the ground. They were as happy as they could be!

Eric and Sam were helping Eric's mother bring in the
laundry when they heard the loud squawking noise again.
"Look!" shouted Eric. "It's the flying Pteranodon!"
"The what?" said his mother.

"The flying Pteranodon!" said Sam.

Eric's mother laughed. "That's not a Pteranodon," she said. "That's a great blue heron."

"Huh?" said Eric.

"A great blue heron," said his mother. "It's a big water bird that you sometimes see flying in the sky."

"But it *can't* be!" cried Eric. "I saw it in my *Big Book About Prehistoric Life.* It's a pterosaur!"

"Did you forget," said his mother, "that pterosaurs are extinct?"

"All of them?" asked Eric.

"Every one," answered his mother.

Eric looked down at the ground. Then he glanced up at
Sam.

"See!" said Sam. "Some Dino Expert *you* are." And Sam
went home.

That night Eric didn't eat much of his supper,

he wasn't interested in the TV special about sea turtles,

and he didn't even smile when his father pretended he was
a Tyrannosaurus rex and tried to chase him into bed.

"I guess I'm not a Dino Expert," said Eric sadly.

"Oh, I don't know," said his mother. "The great blue
heron isn't a Pteranodon, even though it looks a lot like one,
but it just *might* be a living dinosaur!"

"Really?" said Eric.

"Listen to this," said his mother. And she began to read.

"Wow!" said Eric. "Wait until I tell Sam!" And he went to
sleep, feeling much better.

The next morning, on the way to Sam's house, Eric and
his mother stopped at the library.

"Guess what I saw yesterday!" said Eric to Mrs. Williams.

"What?" asked Mrs. Williams.

"A great blue heron," said Eric. "And it might be a living dinosaur!"

"How interesting," said Mrs. Williams.

Just then Sam walked in. But Eric didn't notice. He was too busy talking.

"Yes," said Eric. "It all started with the reptiles, millions and millions of years ago. Then came all the different kinds of dinosaurs."

"How interesting," said Mrs. Williams.

reptile

dinosaurs

Sam moved closer.

"There were some," continued Eric, "called coelurosaurs.
They were small dinosaurs who ran on two legs."

"How interesting," said Mrs. Williams.

Sam moved even closer.

"Some scientists believe," said Eric, "that *these* dinosaurs finally turned into birds—birds like the great blue heron!"

"Wow!" Sam said. "I never knew *that*!"

"I never knew that, either!" said Mrs. Williams.

great blue heron

Archaeopteryx

coelurosaur

"Yes," said Eric. "So that makes the great blue heron a
living dinosaur! And the other birds, too."

"Yikes!" cried Sam. "You *do* know everything! I guess
you really are the Dino Expert!"

"That's for sure!" said Mrs. Williams. "Or, as I like to say,

the budding paleontologist!"

Archaeopteryx fossil

A NOTE TO PARENTS AND TEACHERS

The origin of birds has been debated since at least the 1860s, and it is still being debated by scientists. Many scientists believe that birds are the direct descendants of the dinosaurs. This theory is supported by the discovery in Germany in 1861 of the oldest bird fossil, Archaeopteryx. (It is about one hundred fifty million years old.) Archaeopteryx had the wings and feathers of a bird but a bone structure similar to that of a group of two-legged dinosaurs called coelurosaurs. The fossil led scientists to believe that Archaeopteryx evolved from the coelurosaurs, and that modern birds evolved from Archaeopteryx.

Recently, however, a paleontologist from Texas discovered what he thinks is an earlier bird fossil. It is called Protoavis, and it is about two hundred thirty million years old. This discovery and an even more recent restudy of Archaeopteryx by an ornithologist in North Carolina have challenged the dinosaur-bird connection by instead linking birds to reptiles who lived before the dinosaurs. Nevertheless, the origin of birds is still firmly linked to the dinosaurs in the minds of most paleontologists.

This debate probably will go on for some time to come. Such is the way in which science progresses!